TURTLES

Joanne Randolph

PowerKiDS press™

New York

Published in 2007 by The Rosen Publishing Group, Inc.
29 East 21st Street, New York, NY 10010

First Edition

Book Design: Julio Gil

Photo Credits: Cover, pp. 1, 5, 7, 9, 11, 13, 15, 17, 19, 21 © Shutterstock.com.

Library of Congress Cataloging-in-Publication Data

Randolph, Joanne.
  Turtles / Joanne Randolph. — 1st ed.
       p. cm. — (Classroom pets)
  Includes index.
  ISBN-13: 978-1-4042-3677-6 (library binding)
  ISBN-10: 1-4042-3677-5 (library binding)
  1. Turtles as pets—Juvenile literature. I. Title.
  SF459.T8R36 2007
  639.3'92—dc22
                                                    2006027312

Manufactured in the United States of America

Contents

Picking a Turtle for Your Classroom

Are you ready to meet your new classmate? Turtles can make fun classroom pets. They have special needs, though. Your class needs to do some **research** to decide which kind of turtle is best for your class. You also need to find out what the turtle you pick needs to live a long, happy life.

What kind of home do you need to have ready? What kind of food does the turtle eat? Once you know the answers to these questions, you can start getting ready. Your turtle will thank you for the time you spend!

Some turtles make better pets than others. You want to pick a turtle that is less likely to bite and does not have a lot of special needs.

About Turtles

Turtles are **reptiles**. They have lived on Earth for **millions** of years. In fact, turtles were around when the dinosaurs walked the Earth! Most turtles today live in the warm wet places on Earth. Many have learned to live in colder places, like North America, though. Turtles that live in these colder places **hibernate** in the winter.

Think about the kind of turtle you pick for your classroom. You will need to give the turtle a home that is like the one where it would live in the wild.

These turtles are warming themselves under a sunlamp. Turtles are cold blooded, which means they get their body heat from the heat around them.

So Many Turtles!

In the wild some turtles can live as long as 120 years. That is a long time! Your turtle will not live that long. It will live many years if your class takes care of it, though.

There are many kinds of turtles that can make good pets. Some turtles spend most of their time in the water. The painted turtle, the common snake-necked turtle, and the red-eared slider are just a few of these turtles. Other turtles spend more time on land. Box turtles and painted wood turtles are two turtles that spend more time on land.

Painted turtles are good picks for the classroom. They have colorful markings when they are young that grow lighter as they age.

A Place to Call Home

Each kind of turtle has different needs for its home. Be sure you know what kind of home will make your turtle happy before it comes into your classroom. Some turtles can live in a **terrarium**. Others need an **aquarium**. Almost all turtles like to spend a little time in the water, so you will be safest to use an aquarium for any turtle you pick.

You will need special tools in your turtle's home. The air and water need to be a set **temperature**. You may also need a **filter** to keep the water clean.

Many turtles will need a pool and an island for sunning. The island needs a special light above it to give heat.

Wet or Dry?

Turtles that spend most of their time in the water need more space for a pool. Some like the water to be quiet and still. Others like it to move quickly. Some water turtles like lots of sticks and rocks to help them climb. Other turtles will do better with a smooth bottom.

Turtles that spend more time on land need much less space for a pool. They need more places that are dry, like rocks, logs, sand, and wood chips.

Most turtles also want a place where they can hide in their home.
This turtle is resting among these rocks.

Dinnertime!

Almost all the turtles you would be likely to pick for your classroom are **omnivores**. This means they eat plants and meat. Most turtles like meat best. Feed your adult turtle about every three days.

Be sure your turtle eats enough plants. It also needs fruits, such as apples, blueberries, and bananas. Calcium is important to help keep your turtle's shell healthy. Calcium is something found in foods, like milk and eggshells, that helps bones and teeth stay strong. Your turtle should also take a **vitamin** twice a week.

Turtles need to eat both greens and meat to stay healthy. Always be sure your turtle has plenty of clean water to drink, too.

A Long Winter's Nap

Some turtles need to take a nap for a few months in the winter. This is called hibernation. As days get shorter, you may see that your turtle starts to slow down and eat less. Your pet is getting ready to hibernate. Give the turtle a safe place to spend this time.

Place your turtle in a waterproof box filled with wet moss. Then place the box in a refrigerator that can keep its temperature between 40 and 44° F (4–7° C). You will need to check on your turtle every so often.

For turtles that like to spend most of their time in the water, fill a plastic box with moss and water that is not too deep. You will need to change the water every three to four weeks.

What Does It Mean?

You and your classmates will have lots of fun watching your new pet. Turtles can let you know what they are thinking by the way they act. A turtle that always swims along the wall of its home is likely unhappy. You should check that its home is clean and the turtle has everything it needs.

Sometimes you may see your turtle lying flat with its legs spread out. It is enjoying the sun. If your turtle is standing up tall with its head held high, then it is checking out what is going on around it.

A turtle that has pulled its head and legs into its shell is scared. It will come out of its shell when it feels safe.

A Healthy Pet

It is your job to make sure your turtle stays healthy. Make sure to clean the water in the pool every day. You can also buy a good filter to clean the water. The sand around the swimming pool needs to be kept clean and dry. The sand should be changed every one to two months.

If you think something is wrong with your pet, let your teacher know. Your turtle may have trouble breathing, have puffy eyelids, or have a shell that does not look healthy. These are all reasons to bring your pet to the **veterinarian**.

Be sure to keep the water in your turtle's home clean. Dirty water can make your pet sick.

In the Classroom

Having a turtle for a pet can be great fun. Get to know your new classmate. Think of questions you would like answered about your turtle. Then look up the answers and share them with your class. Everything you learn will help you make a better home for your pet.

Remember that owning a pet is a big job. Your pet is counting on you for everything it needs. Everyone in the class needs to know how to care for the turtle. This way it will be happy whether in your home over a vacation or in the classroom.

Glossary

aquarium (uh-KWAYR-ee-um) A place where animals that live in water are kept for study and show.

filter (FIL-tur) Something that takes out unwanted things from water.

hibernate (HY-bur-nayt) To spend the winter in a sleeplike state.

millions (MIL-yunz) Very large numbers.

omnivores (OM-nih-vorz) Animals that eat both plants and animals.

reptiles (REP-tylz) Animals that breathe air, have scales, or small, hard plates and have body heat that changes with the heat around the body.

research (REE-serch) Careful study.

temperature (TEM-pur-cher) How hot or cold something is.

terrarium (tuh-RER-ee-um) A place for keeping animals and plants inside that does not have standing water.

veterinarian (veh-tuh-ruh-NER-ee-un) A doctor who treats animals.

vitamin (VY-tuh-min) Something taken by mouth to help the body fight illness and grow strong.

Index

A

aquarium, 10

B

box turtles, 8

C

common
   snake-necked
   turtle, 8

F

filter, 10, 20
food(s), 4, 14

L

land, 8, 12

O

omnivores, 14

P

painted turtle, 8
painted wood turtles,
  8

R

red-eared slider, 8
reptiles, 6
research, 4

T

temperature, 10, 16
terrarium, 10
tools, 10

V

veterinarian, 20
vitamin, 14

W

water, 8, 10, 12, 20
wild, 6, 8, 16
winter, 6, 16

Web Sites

Due to the changing nature of Internet links, PowerKids Press has developed an online list of Web sites related to this book. This site is updated regularly. Please use this link to access the list:
www.powerkidslinks.com/cpets/turtle/